KV-261-216

Brilliant Billy DOES HIS BIT

Simon Hutton

Illustrated by Caroline Glicksman

ANDERSEN PRESS
LONDON

Chapter One

All week at school, Billy had been learning about the war, and today a man called Mr. Hoe had come in to tell them all about it.

'Who likes sweets?' Mr. Hoe asked.

Sweets! Billy thrust a hand into the air. The last man to come into class had been dressed as Father

Christmas, and he'd given out chocolate money. But Mr. Hoe was no Father Christmas.

'Sweets are off the menu, I'm afraid. It's fresh vegetables or nothing.' The whole class let out a groan.

'What about fruit?' Billy suggested.

The rest of the class giggled. Billy frowned. Of course sweets were better than fruit, but fruit was fine in an emergency, wasn't it?

Mr. Hoe smiled at him. 'Something sweet, like a banana?' he suggested, obviously catching

Billy's drift. Billy nodded eagerly. But Mr. Hoe shook his head.

'If you want a banana, you have to make it yourself.'

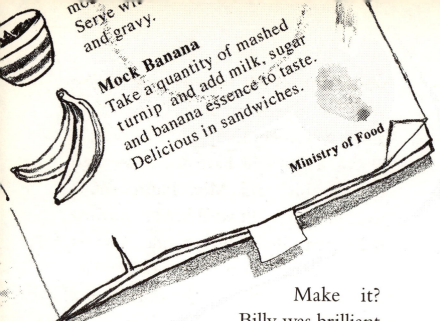

mo...
Serve w...
and gravy.

Mock Banana
Take a quantity of mashed
turnip and add milk, sugar
and banana essence to taste.
Delicious in sandwiches.

Ministry of Food

Make it?
Billy was brilliant
at making things, but
he'd never made a
banana.

'Mash up some turnips, and
add banana essence,' Mr. Hoe told
the class. 'Better than the real thing, in
my opinion. In fact, I still eat them like
that to this day.'

You even had to grow the turnips
first, Billy learned. Everyone had to
grow their own vegetables when there

was a war on. It was part of 'doing your bit', which meant helping out in any way you could.

'We'll soon all have the chance to do our bit,' said Miss Plum, Billy's teacher. 'I thought we'd hold a wartime street party in the playground. A street party is where people bring their tables and chairs and set them up outside, and everybody brings food and drink to share. Mr. Hoe is going to bring one of his prize turnips from his allotment, and I'd like you children to bring along something, too – maybe you'd even like to try growing your own vegetables.'

That was what Billy would do! He was brilliant at

growing things!

He started planning it all out in his head, when someone asked Mr. Hoe when the war had ended.

What a silly question! The war ended when the soldiers stopped fighting, of course!

So Billy was surprised when Mr. Hoe said that for some people, the war had never ended.

'I think what Mr. Hoe means is that for some people, the war was so horrible they can never forget it,' said Miss Plum.

But Billy wasn't so sure. Perhaps Miss Plum just wanted them to think the war was over. After all, war was all about fighting, and she might be worried it would upset them. It certainly upset Miss Plum. You only had to pinch the person next to you and she'd shout.

If the war was over, why were they having a street party?

And if the war was over, why was Mr. Hoe still making his own bananas?

Chapter Two

As soon as he got home, Billy dashed out to the shed to fetch a broom. Defending your borders was the first thing you did in a war,

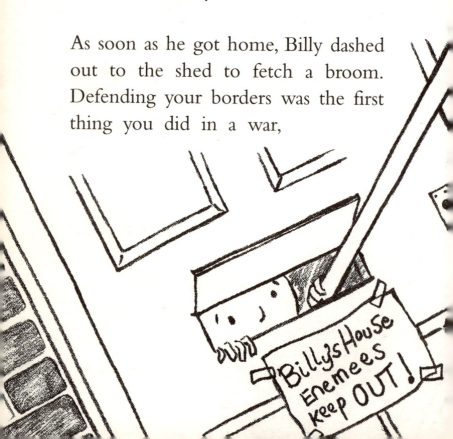

Billys House
Enemees
keep OUT!

Mr. Hoe said, and Billy took up guard behind the front door. The broom was his rifle and he thrust it through the letterbox, daring the enemy to show his face. On the outside of the door, he'd put up a warning sign.

He would watch and wait, and if an enemy came, he would shout, 'Who goes there?'

Nobody came. Not for ages. It began to look like the danger of invasion had passed.

Then suddenly there was a shuffle of footsteps from outside. It was the enemy!

'Who goes there?' Billy called out, gripping his

rifle tightly.

But the enemy took no notice. Instead the enemy pushed open the front door! Billy scrambled backwards just in time. He hoisted his rifle to his shoulder.

'Stop, or I'll shoot!'

There in front of Billy, standing black against the daylight, was a man with a carrier bag in each hand.

'Show me your papers!' Billy ordered. He wasn't sure what papers, but you had to ask for them. Mr. Hoe said.

'I can't show you my papers. My hands are full.'

An enemy trick, thought Billy. 'Put the bags

BAWTRY
TEL: 710858

4/09
- 7 SEP 2009
13 OCT 2016
2 9 AUG 2019
- 2 JUL 2010
3 1 MAY 2011
2 1 JUN 2011
1 2 JUL 2011
1 7 MAR 2012
0 5 APR 2012
- 9 DEC 2014
0 8 OCT 2015
0 6 OCT 2015

Doncaster
Metropolitan Borough Council

DONCASTER LIBRARY AND INFORMATION SERVICES

Please return/renew this item by the last date shown.
Thank you for using your library.

InPress 0231 May 06

3012202259449 9

DONCASTER LIBRARY AND INFORMATION SERVICE	
3012202259449 9	
Askews	20-Apr-2009
	£4.99

First published in Great Britain in 2009 by
ANDERSEN PRESS LIMITED
20 Vauxhall Bridge Road
London SW1V 2SA
www.andersenpress.co.uk

All rights reserved. No part of this publication may be reproduced, stored in a retrieval
system or transmitted in any form, or by any means, electronic, mechanical,
photocopying, recording or otherwise, without the written permission of the publisher.

The rights of Simon Hutton and Caroline Glicksman to be identified as the author and
illustrator of this work have been asserted by them in accordance with the Copyright,
Designs and Patents Act, 1988.

Text copyright © Simon Hutton, 2009
Illustration copyright © Caroline Glicksman, 2009

British Library Cataloguing in Publication Data available.

ISBN 978 184 270 855 2

Printed and bound in Great Britain by CPI Bookmarque, Croydon CR0 4TD down – slowly.'

The man put his bags down. Slowly.

'What's in them, anyway?'

'A surprise.'

'I don't like surprises,' said Billy, who actually loved surprises, but not while he was a soldier. 'A surprise could

mean a bomb or something.'

'Not in this case,' said the man. 'This is a pleasant surprise.'

'What sort of pleasant surprise?' asked Billy, his grip on his rifle slackening.

'Well, if I told you, it wouldn't be a surprise, would it?'

Billy tried to peep. 'But it is pleasant?'

'Of course it's pleasant. Look, Billy, can I come in now?' Dad asked.

'All right – but quick, before any enemies come,' and Billy hustled Dad inside and slammed the door shut.

'I don't know about enemies, but you'll have the whole street poking their noses in while you've got that sign up outside,' said Dad, turning his back on Billy and heading for the kitchen.

Billy waited until Dad was gone before checking outside. Dad was right. The sign was supposed to be warning people away, not making them stop out of curiosity. He'd have

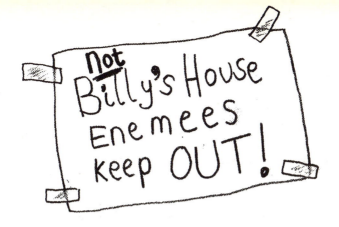

to change it.

That was better. Now enemies would just stroll past without a second glance. It was a brilliant tictac, as Mr. Hoe would say. Or was that 'tactic'?

Billy settled back to his guard duty. This time, no one came. He almost wished someone would. It would take his mind off how hungry he was becoming. He began to dream of burger and chips . . . Burger and chips . . .

His tummy rumbled.

Come on, Mum, give the order!

His tummy whined. His tummy

grumbled.

'Billy! Time for tea!'

At last! Billy threw down the broom and dashed for the kitchen.

Burger and chips!

Burger and chips!

Burger and . . . vegetables?

He stumbled to a halt in the kitchen doorway. No burger. No chips.

They were having vegetables – and *Dad* was cooking them! What was going on?

'A hearty meal for healthy appetites,' Dad was saying. Billy stepped in and circled the table cautiously. Now he could guess what had been in those bags, and it was worse than any bomb.

'A gift from Nature,' said Dad. 'Nothing added and nothing taken away – except the bad bits.'

'Must have been a lot of bad bits,' said Mum. She was at the table gazing into the dishes, which weren't very

full. 'There's hardly anything left. Talk about tiny portions.'

Billy's ears pricked up. Getting tiny portions was called 'rationing'. It was how you shared out food when there wasn't very much. You always got rationing in wars.

'It's quality, not quantity,' said Dad, spooning the vegetables onto plates. 'You don't get food like this at the supermarket.'

'You certainly don't,' said Mum in a wistful voice. She was poking at something small and black amongst the greens. Something with legs. 'Must you grow your own vegetables?'

'Everyone has to,' Billy piped up, remembering what Mr. Hoe had said.

He felt Mum and Dad turn to look at him.

'We've all got to do our bit,' he

added.

Now Mum and Dad were looking at each other, confused.

Dad shrugged. 'Well, at least somebody seems to appreciate my efforts.'

'Then perhaps that somebody should help you down at the allotment,' said Mum. 'At this rate we'll be going hungry.'

Rationing. Allotments. Going hungry. Now Billy was sure there was a war on!

His family needed him – his country needed him. This was his chance to do his bit and Billy knew what he had to do. He was going to grow his own vegetables, the biggest and best vegetables in the whole wide world!

Chapter Three

Billy was brilliant at growing things.
At Cubs, he'd earned a science

badge for raising
cress in a plastic cup.
At school, he'd
cultivated a runner

bean on nothing but cotton wool and water.

And at home, he'd learnt that if you plant an onion, you get an onion. The same onion, as it turns out, but not everyone knew that, did they? That was the kind

of knowledge reserved for experts.

'Now, you know about the different types of veg, don't you, Billy?' Dad asked when they got to the allotment.

Of course he knew. There was frozen veg and canned veg and fresh veg. He knew all about it.

'And you know what allotments are?'

'Of course I do.'

Mr. Hoe had explained. An allotment was a little patch of land where you grew your vegetables. Everyone had an allotment when there was a war on.

Their allotment was in the middle of lots of others. Billy glanced around him and found the ground crawling with men in their wellies, all digging and planting and watering.

'There's one thing you don't know, and I have to tell you before we begin,' said Dad. 'Follow me.'

Billy followed Dad into the shed. It was dark, and smelled of mud. Billy gazed around him at shelves cluttered

with all sorts of gardening things.

There were pots, and bags of compost.

There were tools, and a thing called a dibber, which looked like a wooden

carrot.

But the most important thing, Dad said, was the big bottle on the top shelf.

'Weed killer. And it's not just

harmful to weeds. It's dangerous for small boys, too. I'm only showing you because I don't want you touching it. Top shelf. Weed killer. Don't touch. Got that? Not the top shelf.'

'Weed killer. Not the top shelf,' Billy repeated.

'You've got it,' said Dad, and he turned to leave.

Billy stayed rooted to the spot. 'Which bottle is it again?'

Dad paused and looked at Billy with a puzzled expression. 'It doesn't matter which bottle it is.'

'But they all look the same.'

'Just don't touch any of them.'

'They should have labels,' said Billy sensibly. 'So they don't get mixed up.'

'I know which one's which,' said Dad, making excuses.

'Which one is it, then?' asked Billy.

Dad sighed. 'Just don't touch anything on the top shelf in case it is weed killer. Not the top shelf, OK?'

'Weed killer. Not the top shelf,' Billy said again.

'Good. You make sure you remember that. Weed killer's dangerous stuff – no telling what would happen if it fell into the wrong hands . . .'

Chapter Four

Big vegetables needed big holes, Billy
decided, so he got straight to work.

He dug.

And he dug.

And he *dug*.

In no time at all, he was down to his
knees. Actually it was a long time, and it
was more his ankles than his knees, but
Billy felt like he'd dug to the centre of
the earth! He was aching all over. He
was just about to carry on when a loud
singing voice interrupted him.

"You and me together, we'll win this war forever. Standing tall, never fall, we will not surrender . . ."

Billy looked up to find a face smiling down at him. It was Mr. Hoe – the man Miss Plum had invited into class.

'Digging for victory, are we? What are you planting?'

Billy hadn't thought that far ahead. It didn't much matter what he planted – he was so brilliant at gardening, he could throw anything into the ground and it would thrive.

31

'Peas,'
he said, picking
the first thing that
came into his head.

'I don't think so! Peas
don't need a great big hole
like that.'

'Tomatoes, then,' said Billy,
picking something else at
random.

Mr. Hoe looked at Billy like
he was mad. 'A tomato's a fruit,
young man, not a vegetable.'

How could it be a fruit?
Fruit was apples and
bananas and things like
that. Come to think of
it, bananas were in
short supply –

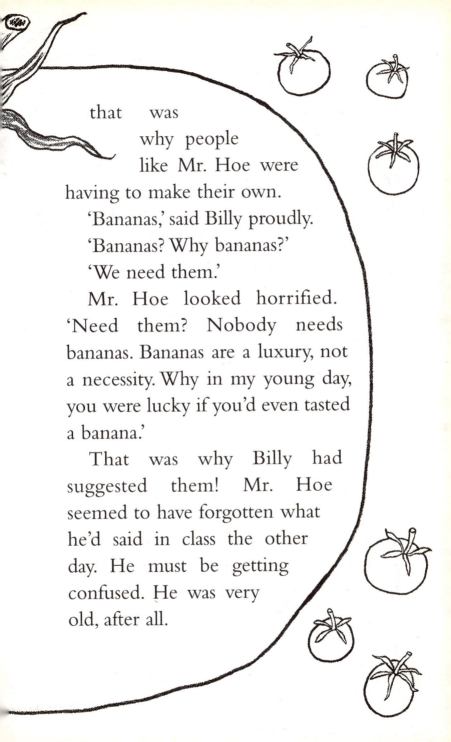

that was
why people
like Mr. Hoe were
having to make their own.

'Bananas,' said Billy proudly.

'Bananas? Why bananas?'

'We need them.'

Mr. Hoe looked horrified. 'Need them? Nobody needs bananas. Bananas are a luxury, not a necessity. Why in my young day, you were lucky if you'd even tasted a banana.'

That was why Billy had suggested them! Mr. Hoe seemed to have forgotten what he'd said in class the other day. He must be getting confused. He was very old, after all.

'What you need to grow is a proper vegetable, something substantial and versatile,' said Mr. Hoe.

Yes, but which vegetable? Billy

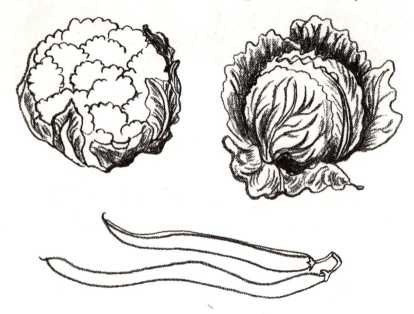

knew them all – from cabbages to cauliflowers to runner beans, but knowing so many just made it harder to pick one.

'What are you growing?' he asked

Mr. Hoe.

Mr. Hoe hooked his thumbs into his jacket button holes. 'Turnips.'

Mr. Hoe must be making another

batch of bananas, Billy thought. He turned a thoughtful eye to his giant hole, which was apparently no good for peas or tomatoes. 'Do turnips grow in the ground?'

'Of course they do! Don't you know that?'

'Yes,' said Billy, who didn't know for certain.

'I shouldn't bother, though,' said Mr.

Hoe. 'No one grows turnips like I do. If you're looking to steal the limelight at this street party, you'll be in for a disappointment.'

Billy wasn't interested in competing against Mr. Hoe – not when there was a whole war to be won. He just wanted to do his bit. But turnips did sound like a good thing to grow. And the bigger he managed to grow them, the more there'd be to go round.

He took a deep breath, his chest swelling with purpose.

'If you're growing turnips, I'll grow

turnips, too. I'm going to grow them as big as I can. After all, we are at war ...'

Chapter Five

Mr. Hoe's eyes widened, then narrowed into slits. He must have thought Billy was challenging him. 'War, eh? Well, we'll see who wins . . .'

Mr. Hoe stopped being quite so friendly after that. And he began hovering. He hovered the way Billy did in the kitchen when Mum just wanted to get on.

If Billy went to the shed, Mr. Hoe would watch him.

If Billy dug a hole, Mr. Hoe would be peeping across the allotment at him.

When Billy started planting his turnip seeds, Mr. Hoe wasted no time in poking his nose in.

'Are you exactly six inches from ground level?'

What did it matter how high he was? It sounded an odd thing to be worrying about. On the other hand, Mr. Hoe was supposed to be good at growing turnips. Perhaps he knew something about it that no one else did. Billy decided to listen. After all, even an expert could sometimes learn

something new.

The trouble was, Billy had no idea how high six inches was. Feet and inches were so confusing. He switched his brain into computer mode. He knew that a 'foot' was how long your foot was, if you were a grown-up. He also knew that inches were smaller than feet. Since children were smaller than grown-ups, perhaps an inch was how long your foot was if you were a child.

He lifted his leg and squinted through one eye at his foot, trying to imagine it six times longer. He raised his hand to chest height. That looked about right.

How could he raise himself that high? There was an old stool in the shed, but he couldn't fetch it without moving his hand. And if he moved his

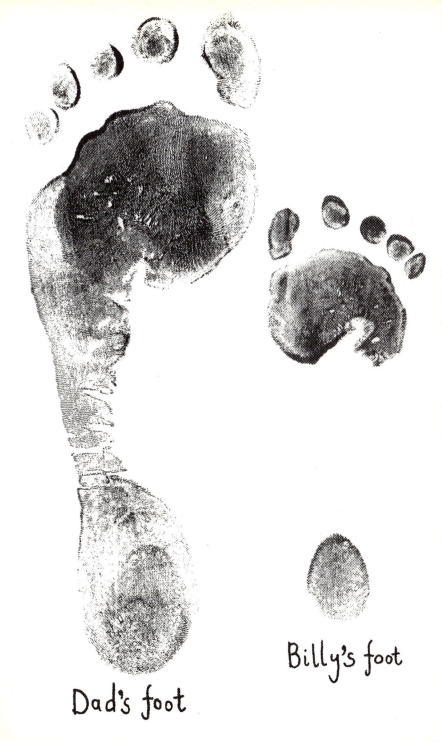

Dad's foot

Billy's foot

hand, he'd lose how high he had to be.

'Mr. Hoe, will you lend me a hand?'

'What do you want a hand with?' asked Mr. Hoe.

'Oh, by itself will be fine,' said Billy (his brain still in computer mode). 'I just need you to put it where mine is.'

Mr. Hoe held out his hand next to Billy's and watched, bemused, as Billy went to the shed and came back with a stool. His eyes widened as Billy climbed up and lay face down to begin scraping at the earth with his fingertips.

'It's no good. My arms aren't long enough.'

'What are you doing?'

'You said I had to be six inches

from ground level.'

'I meant below ground level!'

'Oh.' Billy climbed off the stool and went to lie down in the dirt. Mum would go mad when she found out, but with a war on, sometimes you had to fight dirty.

'Not you! The seeds!' bellowed Mr. Hoe. 'Put the seeds in the ground – this deep,' and Mr. Hoe plucked a pencil from his pocket and held it upright.

Billy pushed himself up on his elbows. That wasn't six inches! It was more like no inches. He might as well sprinkle the seeds on top of the ground, for all the difference it would make.

So that was exactly what Billy did.

Chapter Six

Which is why Billy came to find Mr. Hoe hovering again the next morning, shaking his head in disapproval.

Billy guessed the bad news straight away. The seeds that he'd so carefully and lovingly chucked all over the place were gone. He dropped to his knees to begin a fingertip search, but the earth was bare. Every seed had disappeared.

'No good poking around down there,' rumbled Mr. Hoe. 'You need to look higher to find your culprit.'

Billy raised a disappointed look to Mr. Hoe. How could he do this? With a war on, people were supposed to be helping each other, not being horrible.

'I don't mean me! I mean them! Birds, boy! They're your culprits. Look to the skies!'

Billy glanced up, where he spotted some black specks making lazy circles high above. Three of the black specks broke off and swooped to the ground.

Then suddenly, he saw Mr. Hoe begin to run around the allotment, making pecking movements with his head and flapping his arms up and down.

He thinks he's a bird, thought Billy. He's trying to fly. He's gone crazy.

It was only when they flew off that Billy realised Mr. Hoe was trying to scare the birds, not be one.

Mr. Hoe came to rest, puffing and panting. 'They won't be back for a while. Know your enemy, young man – that's the secret. We're fighting a war here.'

'Will you scare the birds for me again?' Billy asked.

'I've just done it. They're gone.'

'I don't mean now,' said Billy. 'I mean when I'm not here.'

'I can't spend every day running around your allotment!'

'Neither can I,' said Billy. 'I've

got school.'

Mr. Hoe's mouth fell open.

'I can do the weekends if you can do the other days,' Billy offered.

Mr. Hoe began to splutter as if his mouth were full of dirt.

'You'll have to get someone else to do your scaring!'

Billy's shoulders slumped. 'I can't think of anyone.'

Mr. Hoe puffed himself up importantly. 'There's more than one way to win a war,' he said. 'You can either fight your enemy off, or you can trick him.' Billy looked at Mr. Hoe blankly. The old man rolled his eyes. 'A decoy, young man! A blimp! Something that looks like you, but isn't you. A scarecrow . . .'

Billy's scarecrow on
Saturday

Billy's scarecrow
on Sunday

Chapter Seven

'What went wrong?' asked Dad.

Billy shrugged. 'I think probably my scarecrow wasn't scary enough.'

The scarecrow was a sorry sight. And to think that he'd started out so handsome. His back was Billy's broom, and his shoulders were a coat hanger stuck on with sellotape. Billy had drawn a face on a pink balloon, and finished the whole lot off with his school clothes.

Now the scarecrow's head had been popped. It dangled from the top of the broom like a long pink tongue. And the birds had left their droppings all over Billy's school clothes.

'It's a good job there's no school today,' said Billy.

'Yes, but what about tomorrow?'

'Mr. Hoe says we can't tell what tomorrow will bring.'

'I'll tell you what tomorrow will

bring,' said Dad. 'It will bring your mum. She'll be down on you like a ton of bricks — and me, too, for letting this happen.'

Billy shrugged. 'It's the fortunes of war.'

'The what?' said Dad, giving Billy a sharp look.

'Mr. Hoe says you have to take it on the chin. The enemy's adaptable. You have to adapt with him.'

'What enemy?'

'The birds,' said Billy, as if it were obvious.

Dad took a long look at Billy and sighed. 'I think I'm going to have to put an end to this. You're at this allotment practically every night. You're overdoing it.'

'Mr. Hoe says "no pain, no gain",' Billy mumbled.

'Mr. Hoe, Mr. Hoe! Listen, Billy, if you're going to take advice, don't take it off an old duffer like Hoe. Listen to your own feelings. Try imagining you're a plant yourself. What would make *you* grow?'

Food, thought Billy . . .

Chapter Eight

Cola. Cola was perfect for everything. For picnics, for school trips, for drinking at home. Everyone loved cola. Plants couldn't be much different. Cola even looked like plant food, all brown and runny.

Glug glug glug. Into the bowl. The only thing

was, cola was a bit too runny by itself.
Mum always said you needed good
solid food to grow up strong, and there
was nothing very solid about Billy's
Magic Plant Food with only cola in it.
It needed something to make it
thicker.

Crisps were the answer. Crisps were
the answer to everything. They were as
popular as cola. Find someone –
anyone – who doesn't like crisps.

Billy pulled over a chair to reach the
high kitchen cupboard where Mum

kept the treats.

Pickled Onion or Ready Salted? You couldn't expect plants to eat Pickled Onion flavoured crisps. That would be plants eating plants – and that would make them cannibals. Billy picked the red packet.

And chucked it onto the floor.

And jumped on top of it.

And kept on jumping until the crisps inside were reduced to powder.

That powder made a lovely fizz when Billy tipped it into the cola.

Just one ingredient left.

What went with every kind of

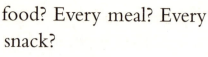

food? Every meal? Every snack?

Ketchup.

Ketchup on chips. Ketchup on burgers. Ketchup in sandwiches. Ketchup was the icing on the cake. In fact, ketchup on cake!

Gloop!

Billy emptied the whole bottle into the bowl and gave the mixture a glorious stir. It looked gorgeous. It tasted gorgeous. It smelt gorgeous. His turnips would be the happiest turnips in the world. And happy turnips meant healthy turnips. It was going to be a bumper harvest!

Chapter Nine

Sure enough, Billy's Magic Plant Food started showing results the very next day. It wasn't magic for nothing!

Of course, it wasn't really magic at all, and anyone else would have been suspicious of how quickly it had acted. But Billy was so excited, he couldn't see it.

As soon as he spotted the little green crown of leaves poking up through the earth, his common sense deserted him and he dropped to his knees and yelled for Dad.

Dad glanced across the allotment, before turning away with a knowing smile. It was Mr. Hoe who came bounding over.

'Look at it!' Billy cried, scraping handfuls of earth away. In front of him was a beautiful, big turnip.

'Quite a specimen,' said Mr. Hoe in an envious voice.

'It's well big!'

'Big enough to take pride of place at the street party.'

Billy's mouth dropped open.

'Except the street party isn't for days. By which time this turnip won't be "well big" at all.'

Billy's mouth clamped shut.

It would be all shrivelled by then, he realised. He ought to dig it up now so they could all enjoy eating it. That was the best way of doing your bit. What did he care about a street party? Except, now he had proof he was a brilliant gardener, he'd quite like the world to know about it. He could show off his turnip at the street party and then they could all eat it. If only it would keep.

'I have an idea,' said Mr. Hoe. 'Why don't you give the turnip to me, and I'll pop it in my freezer? You can have it back on the day of the street party, in perfect condition.'

'You would do that for me?' asked Billy.

'Well, as you said yourself, we all have to, er, do our bit.'

'And you're sure you won't mind?'

'Mind? Of course not. It will be a privilege to own – I mean, to look after – such a fine turnip. I just wish I could grow my turnips as large. You must have green fingers.'

Billy held out his hands. They were brown from digging. And a little red, too, from the ketchup in his Magic Plant Food. But there wasn't a trace of green. He should have thought about that. Mum always said you needed greens to grow up big and strong, and it must be the same for plants.

'I should have added some sprouts. Or cabbage,' said Billy. 'They're green.'

'Added them to what?'

'To my Magic Plant Food.'

'Your magic plant food?'

'That's what made my turnip grow so enormous,' Billy said eagerly.

'Plant food did that?' Mr. Hoe sounded doubtful.

Billy nodded. 'It's well good. It's

only got three ingredients. They're . . .'

Mr. Hoe thrust up a hand for silence.

'Don't utter another word. "Walls have ears", as the saying goes. You don't know who could be listening.'

Billy gulped. 'You don't mean . . . spies?' Billy knew all about spies. Spies were people who spied on you. They

watched what you were doing and reported back to the enemy. You always got spies in wars.

Mr. Hoe gave a sombre nod. 'Promise me that you've got your plant food safely hidden away.'

Billy hesitated. With spies listening, whatever he said next would be reported back. The enemy would learn the location of his plant food and steal it!

Then he remembered something Mr. Hoe had said. There was more than one way to win a war. You could either fight your enemy – or you could trick him. Billy smiled inwardly. A beautiful tactic was forming in his mind.

He would give the spies something to report back, all right – but it wouldn't be what they wanted. He wouldn't exactly lie (he didn't like lying, not even to spies) but he wouldn't exactly tell the truth, either.

'My Magic Plant Food is in the shed, on the top shelf,' he announced in a voice loud enough for the spies to overhear.

Mr. Hoe frowned. 'The top shelf is where the weed killer's kept, surely?'

Billy shook his head. '"Weed killer. Not the top shelf",' he said, repeating what Dad had made him practise. Every word was the truth. Kind of. He tried to wink at Mr. Hoe, but it came out as a blink instead. It didn't matter though, because Mr. Hoe seemed to have caught on anyway. Billy watched him tap the side of his nose knowingly.

'Just so we're clear. Wouldn't want a mix up, would we?'

Of course not, thought Billy, trying not to giggle as he imagined the

enemy stealing weed killer instead of
plant food . . .

Chapter Ten

'Looks like my plan worked,' Dad whispered to Mum later that day. Billy was in the other room, watching the children's programmes on TV. Gardening seemed to be the last thing on his mind. 'Billy thinks he's grown a monster turnip, and he's given the gardening a rest. He's happy – and we're happy. Everyone's happy!'

And everyone stayed happy. In fact, Billy got happier and happier as each day passed. When the day of the street

party finally came, he was on top of the
world, and nothing could bring him
down. Or so he thought.

The school playground was like a film set. There were tents and marquees, and tables loaded with food. There were people in costume. There was bunting everywhere, and children were waving flags. Even Miss Plum had made a special effort. She was dressed in old-fashioned clothes and was wearing a headscarf and bright red lipstick.

A brass band was playing the same song Billy had heard Mr. Hoe singing.

'That's called *We'll Win This War*,' said Billy

knowledgeably.

'Well done, Billy!' said Miss Plum, her red lips making her smile glow. 'You're certainly getting into this whole "war" thing.'

'It's not the only thing he's been getting into,' said Mum. 'We've had gardening, day and night.'

'Billy doesn't do things by half,' Dad added.

They came to the table holding the

vegetable display. There was every kind of vegetable imaginable. And in the middle of them all, shining like a diamond in a crown, was Billy's turnip, freshly defrosted.

'There it is,' Billy whispered to Mum and Dad proudly. He always knew he could grow a giant turnip if he tried. Now he knew he could grow a giant turnip even if he didn't try!

He'd done his bit, all right.

Mum and Dad were obviously proud, too. Mum was hugging him, and Dad was so proud he was biting his bottom lip, obviously overcome with emotion.

Miss Plum stepped up to the table. 'So, these are the vegetables from the allotments?'

Mr. Hoe appeared from nowhere, bobbing up on his toes and giving a nod.

'And whose is this wonderful turnip in the middle? I don't think I've ever seen anything quite so big.'

Billy stepped forward, beaming.

At which point, Mr. Hoe took a step forward, too.

Billy took another step.

Mr. Hoe took another step.

'Stop following me, boy!' Mr. Hoe

barked.

'But you're following me!'

'I'm not following anyone! I'm going up to show your teacher my turnip.'

'Your turnip? But that's my turnip!

I grew it myself!'

'Sorry, have to speak up. Bit deaf. It grew by

itself, you say?'

No, he hadn't said that! And before he could say anything at all, Mr. Hoe moved forward. Billy could only stare in disbelief as Mr. Hoe went to take the credit for his turnip.

Chapter Eleven

'What lovely colours,' said Miss Plum, stroking the surface of the turnip.

Mr. Hoe smiled with satisfaction.

Billy stood with his mouth hanging open. This couldn't be happening!

'There are greens and oranges and purples and . . . a little square of white?' Miss Plum frowned.

Mr. Hoe's smile fell from his face.

Miss Plum began to pick at the little square of white with her thumb

nail. The square peeled off.

'It's a price sticker!' Miss Plum glared at Mr. Hoe. It was a look she usually reserved for naughty children. 'Mr. Hoe! You didn't buy this turnip from a supermarket, did you?'

'No, I didn't! *He* did!' Mr. Hoe jabbed a finger at Billy.

'Billy, you bought it from a supermarket?'

'No, I didn't!' Billy wailed. Now he was thoroughly confused. He'd dug that turnip up with his own hands. Perhaps the sticker had come from something else in Mr. Hoe's freezer.

'I bought the turnip from the supermarket,' said Dad, stepping in at that moment and hoisting the turnip from Miss Plum's hands. 'Dinner tonight. Yum yum. Sorry for the mix-up, everyone.'

Turnip Soup

Ingredients: One very large turnip
One onion
Whatever else you can get
A little fat
One-and-half pints water
Salt and pepper

Method: Chop the vegetables and brown in the fat. Add water, simmer for two hours. Season and serve with slices of National Bread.

Ministry of Food

Ministry

d mutton
nd turnips
ed potatoes
egetable water

s in a casserole.
ed paper and

Chapter Twelve

Billy felt his eyes begin to sting with tears. How humiliating! He hadn't done his bit at all — he'd been cheated out of doing it. And he couldn't even claim to be a brilliant cheater, because it was Dad who'd done the cheating! How could Dad do this to him?

Fortunately, teachers are good at dealing with awkward situations.

'Mix-ups happen,' said Miss Plum in a practical voice. 'Mr. Hoe, why don't you go to your allotment and bring back your best turnip?'

Mr. Hoe glanced up like an excited child and bounded away to do what he was told.

'But Miss Plum . . . ' Billy protested.

Miss Plum held up her finger for silence.

'As for you, Billy, your mum and dad tell me that you've been doing some gardening, too.'

Billy nodded.

'Well then, why don't you go and fetch something that you've been growing?'

Billy didn't move. 'I don't have anything to fetch.'

Miss Plum was not put off. 'You must have something. Remember what we said in class? In a war, everyone has to do their bit, even if what they do is only something very small. So go on – run along.'

Billy didn't run. He shuffled. He sloped. He scraped his feet over the ground as if they were made of stone.

What was the point in hurrying? What was the point in going at all? The moment he'd found that huge turnip, he'd forgotten about everything else on the allotment. He hadn't been back for days. Anything else that had been growing there would be dead by now.

When he reached the allotment, he stood there for a long time, feeling miserable. He gave the earth an angry kick.

When kicking the earth uncovered a leaf, he didn't get excited. He assumed the leaf must have blown there from another allotment.

And when he pulled at the leaf and

found it was attached to a turnip, he felt a rush of hope, before telling himself it must be another of Dad's tricks.

But then he licked his finger, and tasted cola and crisps and ketchup . . .

Chapter Thirteen

Billy clawed at the earth. One, two, three…There were turnips everywhere! They weren't big, but they were beautiful!

He dug out the best one he could find, and bounded back to the school playground. The street party was still in full swing. Everyone was there. Mum. Dad. Miss Plum. No one was missing.

No one except Mr. Hoe. Where was he?

They found him standing over his

vegetable patch. His face had gone white. He was shaking.

'My beautiful turnips . . .'

Turnips? He must mean those rows of wilted green leaves, thought Billy.

'Ruined,' Mr. Hoe groaned. 'Utterly ruined. Nothing can save them.'

Billy knew he shouldn't feel sorry for Mr. Hoe, not after Mr. Hoe had tricked him out of his turnip, but he couldn't

stand by when he knew he could help. There was a war on, and people had to look out for each other. Everyone had to do their bit. Mr. Hoe's turnips just needed a bit of reviving, that was all.

'Why don't you try some of my Magic Plant Food?' he offered.

'What plant food's that, Billy?' asked Dad.

'I made it myself. It's in the shed.'

'I hope you didn't touch the weed killer on the top shelf.'

Mr. Hoe

gave a sudden gasp that made everyone look. 'Weed killer? You put weed killer on the top shelf?'

Dad nodded. 'On the top shelf, where it's out of reach.'

Mr. Hoe's lower lip began to tremble.

'What did I say about the weed killer, Billy?' asked Dad. 'I said, "There's weed killer on the top shelf, so don't touch".'

Billy nodded. He could remember it word for word. He was brilliant at remembering things. 'Weed killer. Not the top shelf.'

'Exactly. Imagine what would happen if you got weed killer mixed up with something else . . . '

Chapter Fourteen

'Did you know that the war was when people's eating habits were at their most healthy?' said Dad later at home. 'It's a fact. No burgers or chips or sweets, you see. No junk food at all. Just lots of healthy vegetables.'

'It won't be good for your health if you've brought back any leftovers from that street party,' Mum warned. 'I've had enough vegetables to last me a lifetime.'

Dad shrugged. 'Well, you know the

old wartime saying, "Waste not, want not".'

Mum shot him a dark look.

'On the other hand, bringing back vegetables might not be good for morale.'

'What's "morale"?' asked Billy.

'Something they often talk about in wars,' said Dad. 'It's how you feel about yourself, whether you feel good or bad. I don't feel too good about myself at all, right at the moment, because I tricked you with that turnip. I am sorry, Billy.'

Billy gave a shrug. 'That's all right. It all worked out well in the end, anyway.'

Dad regarded Billy with admiration. 'That's the kind of spirit that won the war, Billy. I'm proud of you.'

'Anyway,' said Billy, sneaking a sidelong grin in Mum's direction, 'I expect you were under orders.'

Dad began to laugh.

Mum crossed her arms and treated father and son to a glare of mock indignation.

'I don't know why you're making me out to be the villain. I'm not the one who bought turnips from a supermarket and planted them in Billy's vegetable patch.'

'You know, that's the weird thing,' said Dad. 'I only bought one turnip. Billy, I reckon a few of your seeds must have got deep down, away from the birds, and you forgot about them. Either that, or your magic plant food really *is* magic.'

Dad took Billy's hands in his own and turned them over. Muddy. Cut. Cracked nails. 'Whichever way you look at it, these certainly are green fingers. Green fingers are what someone has when they're an expert at gardening.'

Billy looked at his muddy hands and a sudden thought came to him. 'Hey, I know, I can grow all our vegetables now, not just turnips!'

Mum shot a glance

at Dad. Dad thought quickly.

'See, the thing is, Billy, it's like I say – you're an expert at gardening.'

'Exactly!'

'But you know what it is with experts. Experts are people who no longer get their hands dirty.'

'But you can't do gardening and not get your hands dirty,' said Billy.

'Well, that's it, you see. No more dirty hands means no more gardening.'

Billy's shoulders slumped. 'I just wanted to do my bit for the war.'

Dad started to laugh and shake his head. 'Billy, there's no war . . . '

Mum interrupted. 'What Dad means is that the war's over now. There's no need for you to grow food at the allotment any more.'

'No more vegetables for tea?' asked Billy.

'I'm afraid not.'

A sly smile crept onto Billy's face.

'Does that mean we can have bananas?'

'Bananas?'

'*Real* bananas. Not made from turnips.'

'Billy, you can have any sort of banana you like.'

Billy settled back in his chair, his hands behind his head and a smile on his lips. 'I'm glad the war's over,' he sighed.

'We all are,' agreed Dad.

But there was one question still on Billy's mind. He sat up, looking puzzled. 'Who actually won the war?'

Mum smiled. 'You did, Billy.'

'Practically all by yourself,' Dad added. 'You were brilliant.'

IF YOU LOVED THIS, WHY NOT TRY:

Brilliant Billy's BIG Book of Dinosaurs

There's a prize for the best story – and Billy really wants to win it. He'll write about dinosaurs - after all, he's an expert on them! But the harder he tries, the harder he finds it. Will a visit to the dinosaur museum make a difference?

ISBN 9781842705698 £4.99

CHOSEN FOR THE SLA'S BOYS INTO BOOKS LIST